TREEHOUSE RESCUE!

Published by the Penguin Group. Penguin Group (USA) Inc.,
375 Hudson Street, New York, New York 10014, USA.
Manufactured in China

F. WARNE & CO

978-0-7232-8040-8   10 9 8 7 6 5 4 3 2 1

Map of My Woods

This is a map of the woods where I live. You can see who else lives here, too. The map is in my dad's journal, which I always have with me.

ROCKY ISLAND

OLD BROWN'S ISLAND

Old Brown is very bad tempered. We stay away from him.

MR. JEREMY FISHER'S PO

SQUIRREL NUTKIN'S WOOD

MRS. TIGGY-WINKLE'S LAUNDRY

Squirrel Nutkin has some of the best (and nuttiest) ideas.

This is **Mr. Tod**. Foxes eat rabbits. Need I say more?

JEMIMA PUDDLE-DUCK'S HILLTOP FARM

MR. MCGREGOR'S GARDEN

My friend, **Lily Bobtail**. Whatever the problem, she's got the answer.

MR. TOD & TOMMY BROCK'S WOOD

MY BURROW

TUNNEL NETWORK

DR. & MRS. BOBTAIL'S BURROW

MR. BOUNCER'S BURROW (BENJAMIN'S HOME)

RAVINE

DEEP DARK WOODS

DANDELION FIELD

Benjamin Bunny is my cousin. Whatever I do, he's right behind me — usually hiding!

One sunny morning, Peter, Lily, and Benjamin were hopping happily through the woods. Suddenly Peter stopped, sniffed, and rubbed his chin . . .

"Someone's following us!"

Peter spun around, then stood still as a statue. Behind him, Benjamin and Lily trembled with fear. "Don't worry," said Peter. "We'll all stick together."

"Hello, my floppy-eared friends," hissed Mr. Tod, licking his lips.

"MMM! Perfect for a PIE!"

"Quick. Let's hide!" called Peter, dodging Mr. Tod and bounding away.

The friends hopped and hopped, then stopped when Benjamin heard giggling in the trees.

"Lucky squirrels!
It's easy to hide
up there."

"Yes, it is. Great idea, Benjamin!" said Peter.
"If we had a hideout in Squirrel Camp,
Mr. Tod would NEVER find us."

The Camp was VERY high up. Benjamin did NOT enjoy the journey.

Squirrel Nutkin was bouncing around in the branches. He was not at all sure rabbits belonged in trees. "You can't just HAVE a hideout up here," he squeaked importantly.

"First you have to pass three SECRET SQUIRREL TESTS."

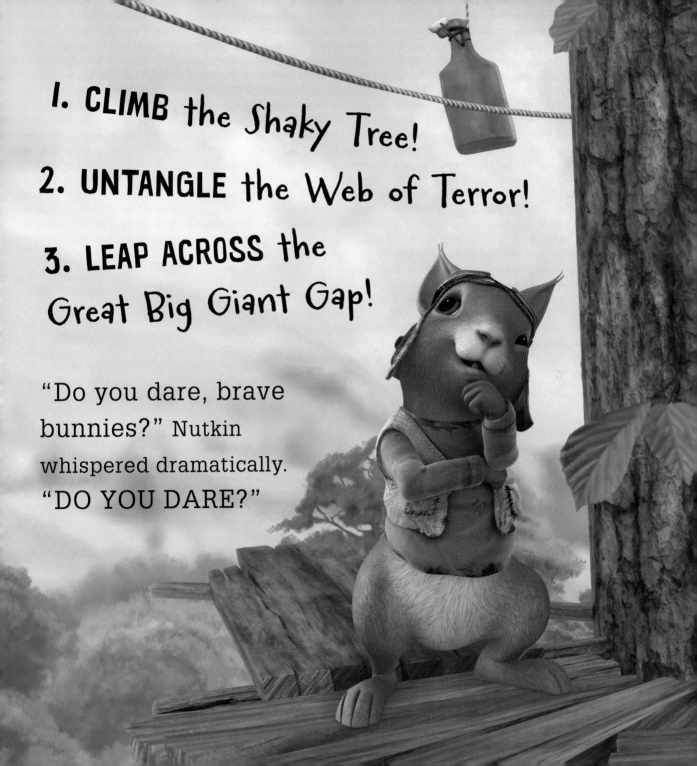

1. **CLIMB** the Shaky Tree!

2. **UNTANGLE** the Web of Terror!

3. **LEAP ACROSS** the Great Big Giant Gap!

"Do you dare, brave bunnies?" Nutkin whispered dramatically. "DO YOU DARE?"

The brave bunnies DID dare.

Benjamin made it up to the top of the Shaky Tree . . . and shook with terror.

"Pass!"

"Well done, Benjamin!"

Lily tiptoed through the tangled Web of Terror.

"I can do this," Lily murmured to herself.

And she was right!

"Pass!"

"Two tests down, and one to go," muttered a determined Peter. "Better hop to it!" He took a deep breath and . . .

"WHEEEEEE!"

"Hopping hazelnuts!"

gasped Nutkin.

"The final test . . .

. . . failed!"

The Great Big Giant Gap was just TOO BIG. "Oh no!" sighed Peter. Luckily, the giggly squirrels caught him in their bucket as he fell and winched him back up.

There was to be no treehouse hideout after all.

The three friends made their way sadly down to the ground in the elevator.

"At least we won't have to listen to those squawking squirrels every day," Lily sighed.

"And it is AWFULLY high up," added Benjamin.

Suddenly the woods were filled with a terrifying SCREECHING sound . . .

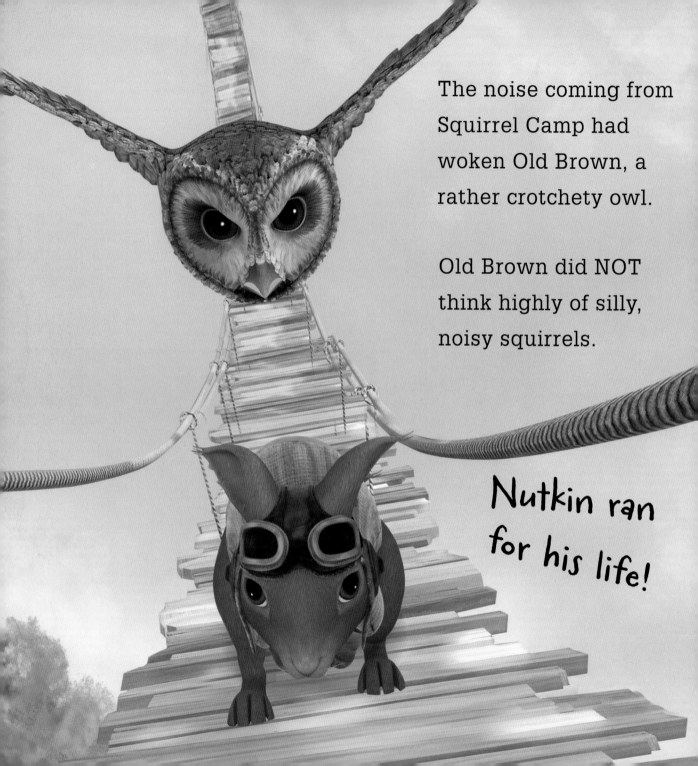

The noise coming from Squirrel Camp had woken Old Brown, a rather crotchety owl.

Old Brown did NOT think highly of silly, noisy squirrels.

Nutkin ran for his life!

"Old Brown is attacking
Squirrel Camp!" yelled Peter.

"We have to get back
up there and help!"

Nutkin was trapped high in the trees
on the other side of the Great Big Giant Gap.

"I've got a plan!" said Peter.
"It's risky, but it just might work."

Dodging panicking squirrels one
way and Old Brown's needle-sharp
talons the other, he and brave
Benjamin . . .
GRABBED
Nutkin's paw . . .

and SWUNG across
the Great Big
Giant Gap . . .

. . . just in time.

"I'll get you next time, tailless tree rat!" Old Brown screeched furiously as he flew away.

"OOOOH. Fabulous flying!"

"Hooray for the brave rabbits!"

And things were about to get even better.

The rabbits watched as Nutkin's assistant chalked
a big check beside the final Squirrel Test.

"Pass!"

"Look at that!"
laughed Peter.
"Maybe rabbits
DO belong in
trees after all!"

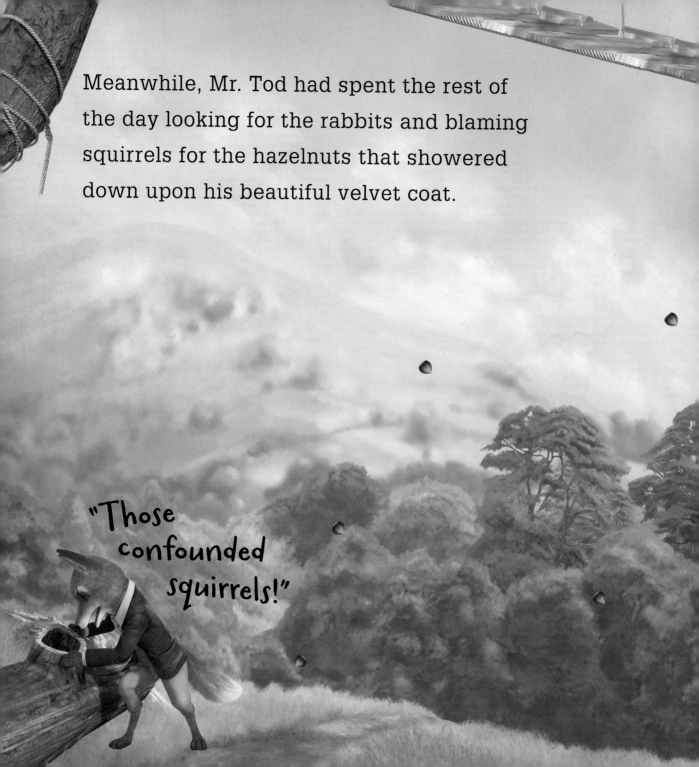

Meanwhile, Mr. Tod had spent the rest of the day looking for the rabbits and blaming squirrels for the hazelnuts that showered down upon his beautiful velvet coat.

"Those confounded squirrels!"

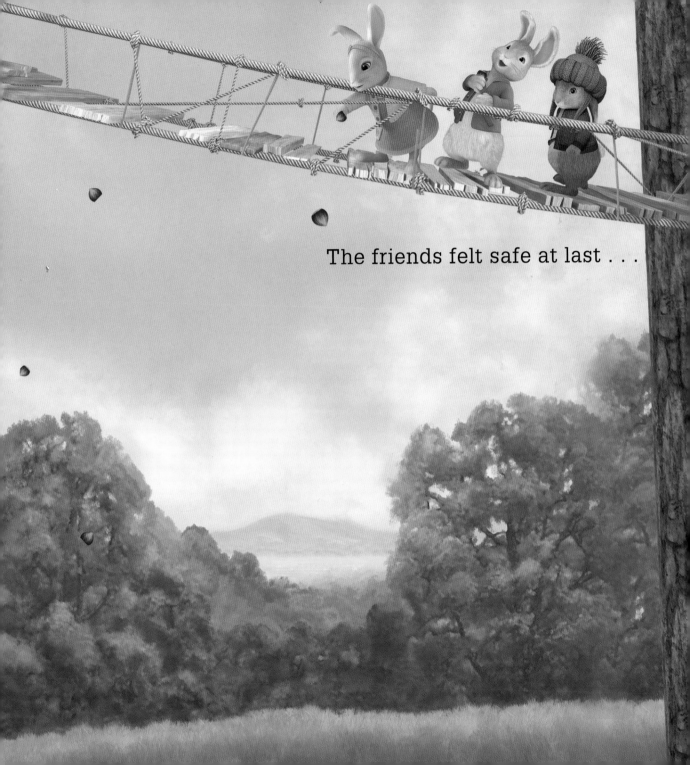

The friends felt safe at last . . .

. . . in their new secret clubhouse.

"This is what I call a good hiding place!" called Peter.

"It's the perfect place to plan new ADVENTURES!"

OUR TREETOP HIDEOUT

Rabbits can't climb trees like squirrels, so we travel up and down in this elevator. Only the squirrels really know how it works, but it's better than brilliant!

Up to Branch Manager's off

Let's Work on Your **WOBBLE!**

Today we're practicing our balancing skills. It's fun doing things together, and we'd love it if you joined in too. It's tricky for rabbits, since we have BIG FEET!

Good balance is important in the sky-high Squirrel Camp!

Benjamin and Lily passed their Squirrel Tests with flying colors.

WHY DON'T YOU TRY THESE?

Stand on one leg for thirty seconds.

Walk along a low wall or a fallen log. (Hold on tight to a grown-up's hand.)

Touch the tip of your nose and walk in a straight line.

Awesome skills, my friend!

CONGRATULATIONS!

SKILL IN BALANCING CERTIFICATE

Awarded to

- -

- -

Age

- -

Squirrel Nutkin
- - - - - - - - - - - - - - - - -
SQUIRREL NUTKIN
BEST BALANCER IN THE WOOD